mary-kateandashley

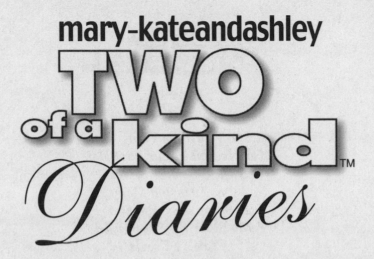

TWO of a kind™ Diaries

Look for these

titles:

1 *It's a Twin Thing*
2 *How to Flunk Your First Date*
3 *The Sleepover Secret*
4 *One Twin Too Many*
5 *To Snoop or Not to Snoop*
6 *My Sister the Supermodel*
7 *Two's a Crowd*
8 *Let's Party!*
9 *Calling All Boys*
10 *Winner Take All*
11 *P.S. Wish You Were Here*
12 *The Cool Club*
13 *War of the Wardrobes*
14 *Bye-bye Boyfriend*
15 *It's Snow Problem*
16 *Likes Me, Likes Me Not*
17 *Shore Thing*

mary-kateandashley

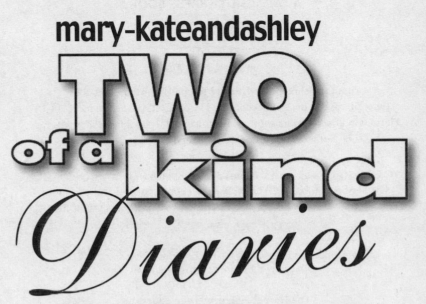

Two of a kind Diaries

Two for the Road

by Nancy Butcher

from the series created by
Robert Griffard & Howard Adler

HarperCollins*Entertainment*
An Imprint of HarperCollins*Publishers*
A PARACHUTE PRESS BOOK

A PARACHUTE PRESS BOOK

Parachute Publishing, L.L.C.
156 Fifth Avenue
Suite 302
New York, NY 10010

First published in the USA by Harper Entertainment 2001
First published in Great Britain by HarperCollins*Entertainment* 2003
HarperCollins*Entertainment* is an imprint of HarperCollins*Publishers* Ltd,
77-85 Fulham Palace Road, Hammersmith, London, W6 8JB

TWO OF A KIND, characters, names and all related indicia are trademarks of
Warner Bros. © 2001. TWO OF A KIND books created and produced
by Parachute Press, L.L.C., in cooperation with Dualstar Publications,
a division of Dualstar Entertainment Group, LCC.,

Cover photo courtesy of Dualstar Entertainment Group, LLC.
© Dualstar Entertainment Group, LLC. 2001

The HarperCollins website address is
www.**fire**and**water**.com

1 3 5 7 9 10 8 6 4 2

The authors assert the moral right to be
identified as the authors of this work

ISBN 0 00 714463 6

Originated by Dot Gradations Ltd, UK

Printed and bound in Great Britian by Clays Ltd, St Ives plc

Chapter 1

Saturday

Dear Diary,

Help! Mary-Kate is missing!

Oh, Diary, I never thought I'd be writing to you with such awful news. Mary-Kate and our friend Phoebe Cahill have been missing all day. They went canoeing in an alligator-filled swamp and never came back. The camp counsellors are organising a search party. I'm in my room, waiting for them to come and get me.

Mary-Kate, Phoebe, and I are in the Florida Keys, in a place called Camp Coral Reef. It's part of a special summer field trip that was arranged by our school, the White Oak Academy for Girls.

There are three other First Formers from White Oak: Summer Sorenson, Cheryl Miller and Elise Van Hook. Plus, there are five First Formers from the Harrington School for Boys: our cousin Jeremy Burke, Seth Samuels, Justin Martinez, Ross Lambert and Devon Benjamin, who's starting at Harrington in the fall. "First Form" is what they call seventh grade at White Oak and Harrington.

1

Camp Coral Reef isn't the sort of camp where you do crafts and play Capture the Flag and sleep on rock-hard bunks. Our "dorm" is this super-cool beach house with wicker furniture and a wrap-around porch that overlooks the ocean. For the last two weeks we've been studying wildlife photography, deep-sea fishing, and scuba-diving.

Anyway, it began right after we got here. Mary-Kate and I made this dumb bet. I happened to say a  few things about scuba, like how diving too deep can make your lungs explode and your eyeballs pop out. And how I wasn't crazy about the idea of being chased by thirty-foot alligators. It's not like I made this stuff up. I got it out of a really scientific book called *The Worst That Can Happen*.

Well, Mary-Kate took all this the wrong way.

"What a wuss!" she said with a laugh. "I bet you're not going to pass your scuba test. I bet you won't even make it through the next few weeks of camp. You'll be too scared to do anything!"

"A wuss?" I gasped. "I am not a wuss! I bet I can totally ace all this camp stuff! Not only that, I'll pass my scuba test . . . the first time!"

We hooked pinkies on that. Mary-Kate said

whoever lost the bet would have to clean the winner's side of her dorm room for six whole months. That seemed a little harsh, especially since her side of the dorm room looks like her wardrobe exploded or something. I was pretty confident I was going to win, though, so I didn't put up too much of a fuss.

But things went downhill after that. *Way* downhill. I got really wrapped up in winning the bet. I also got a tiny bit wrapped up in the new guy, Devon Benjamin. Devon's from Daytona Beach, and he's super-nice, *plus* he's really, really cute. I should never have started thinking about him that way, though. I already *have* a boyfriend: Ross Lambert.

Well, I can't say it was all my fault.

The only person who knew about my Devon crush was Mary-Kate. And guess what? Mary-Kate blabbed my secret to the whole world, and Ross found out!

I got over my crush on Devon really fast. I discovered that we had nothing in common. He doesn't like mint chocolate-chip ice cream, and he doesn't like the band 4-You, either. Some people have no taste!

But Ross didn't get over being mad at me. Mary-Kate and I got into a big fight because of that. I accused her of blabbing my secret because she saw I was winning our bet. Mary-Kate insisted that she was innocent, but I didn't believe her.

Then two days ago she made things even worse between Ross and me. Mary-Kate said she was only trying to help. But I didn't believe that, either.

Mary-Kate and I stopped speaking to each other after that. Actually, that's not true. We stopped speaking to each other *after* I told her that when we got back home to Chicago, I was going to ask Dad for separate rooms because she was a total rat.

Now I know that nothing I accused Mary-Kate of is true. Oh, Diary, how could I have said those terrible things to her? How could I have let this stuff with Ross and Devon come between us? I mean, boys are important, but a sister is for ever.

And now she's missing! We had a big Camp Coral Reef canoe race this morning. Everyone finished by lunchtime – except for Mary-Kate and Phoebe, who didn't finish at all.

Where could they be? Will I ever see my sister again?

Got to go, Diary. Sid Pepper, the camp director, just knocked on my door and said that the search party's ready to roll.

This is *not* the kind of party I had in mind for our last weekend at Camp Coral Reef. Oh, Diary! We have to find them. We just *have* to.

Two for the Road

Dear Diary,

This is probably the last time I'll be writing to you.

Unless someone comes and rescues us, fast!

Diary, you'll never guess where I am. Phoebe and I are stuck on an island in the middle of a swamp. That's why there are little dead mosquitoes smushed all over the page.

Phoebe and I were team-mates in the Camp Coral Reef canoe race. We were doing just great, following the little red flags that Sid and Brad and the other camp counsellors set up for the course.

But then we got to a place in the swamp where there were lots of spiders' webs stretched across the water – like the ones in those fake haunted houses, except these weren't fake. Phoebe said there was no way she was going under the spiders. I kind of agreed with her. So we took a different route.

Big mistake! We paddled and paddled for what seemed like forever. The swamp kept getting narrower and windier and slimier and soupier. We couldn't find any red flags, and we couldn't find any other canoers, either. It seemed as if we were the only ones for miles around.

Finally our canoe jammed into a bunch of mangrove roots. Mangroves are these gnarly trees that grow out of the water. No matter what we did, we couldn't get our canoe loose.

"I think we're stuck," Phoebe gulped.

"And lost!" I declared.

I stood up in the canoe and cupped my hands around my mouth. "Help!" I yelled.

Phoebe joined in. "Heeelllllp!"

But there was no answer.

We finally gave up. We didn't know what else to do, so we aban-doned ship and walked across a giant mangrove root over to this  island. If you can call it that. It's just a big mound of moss and weeds with some bullfrogs, horseshoe crabs, and a whole lot of mosquitoes living on it.

We sat down on a spot that wasn't too slimy.

"If no one finds us soon, we're toast!" Phoebe announced grimly.

"If no one finds us, we're gator chow!" I corrected her. Florida, especially this part of Florida, is full of alligators – and other dangerous creatures, too.

So now we've been sitting here for a long time staring out at the swamp. Once in a while a pelican or a heron swoops down and checks us out. I've been having all sorts of dark, morbid thoughts. Like, even if we *don't* end up being gator chow (or crocodile chow or panther chow), how are we going to survive? I have half a protein bar in my backpack. Phoebe has three breath mints. We have a small bottle of cranberry juice. And I don't see anything to eat or drink on our little island, unless we're in the mood for bullfrog sushi or slimy green swamp water.

"Phoebe?" I said after a while. "Are we going to starve to death?"

"Don't even *say* that!" Phoebe cried out. "We can't give up!"

She jumped to her feet and headed back out to the canoe. She tried to pry it loose. "It's really, really stuck," she called out.

"I think we'd better start making a will," I said miserably. "You know, in case we don't . . . survive. I could write it down in my diary. Maybe someone will find it someday."

Phoebe sat down next to me again. "If something happens to us, I'm going to leave all my vintage black dresses to Ashley," she declared. Phoebe is a vintage *anything* nut and has an amazing collection of old clothes, jewellery, and shoes. Right now she was wearing khaki shorts, a green safari hat, and a pair of Keds madras trainers from the 1960s.

At the mention of Ashley's name, I felt this awful pang. As of this morning, Ashley and I weren't speaking to each other. I was hoping we'd get a chance to make up after the canoe race.

But now I'm not sure we'll ever get the chance!

"I'm going to leave Ashley my Derek Jeter poster, my favourite glove, and all my CDs," I said in a choked-up voice.

"You'd better start writing this stuff down," Phoebe urged.

"O-okay." I turned to a fresh page and started writing:

LAST WILL AND TESTAMENT

WE, MARY-KATE BURKE AND PHOEBE CAHILL, LEAVE THE FOLLOWING ITEMS TO OUR BELOVED FRIENDS AND FAMILY MEMBERS: TO ASHLEY BURKE, PHOEBE LEAVES HER COLLECTION OF VINTAGE BLACK DRESSES, AND MARY-KATE LEAVES HER DEREK JETER POSTER, HER FAVOURITE GLOVE, AND HER ENTIRE CD COLLECTION.

Phoebe read over my shoulder, then started giggling.

"What?" I demanded. "What is so funny about me leaving Ashley my stuff?"

"It's not that," Phoebe said. "I just thought of something we could leave Summer. A dictionary!"

I grinned. "Yeah! If she had a dictionary, she wouldn't get all those hard words mixed up."

"Like *initials* and *initiations*." Phoebe did a perfect imitation of Summer's voice. "'I have a fourteen-carat-gold necklace with my initiations on it! SVS, for Summer Victoria Sorenson!'" We both cracked up.

"We could leave Cheryl a copy of *Cooking 101 for Dummies*, since she's such a bad cook," I suggested. "Remember those brownies she made that time? They tasted like . . . like . . ."

"Baked swamp slime!" Phoebe laughed.

I nodded and wrote it all down, word for word. "Hey, I thought of something we could leave Seth! A subscription to *GuyStyle* magazine, since he wears such geeky clothes!"

"And don't forget Ross! We could leave him a dartboard with Devon Benjamin's picture on it!"

We went on like this for a long time. I was writing like mad, recording it all. I know we were

9

saying some pretty mean things about our friends. But it made us laugh.

I heard a noise. It sounded like . . . thunder. I glanced up at the sky. It had got really dark. A storm was coming!

I stared at the dark sky, and at the murky green  swamp, and at our canoe that was totally stuck in the mangroves. I realised that more than anything, at that moment, Phoebe and I needed to laugh.

I was just about to tell Phoebe what we should leave my cousin Jeremy when we heard *another* noise. A splashing noise.

I just heard the noise again. It sounds like something coming towards us in the water.

It sounds like an alligator!

Chapter 2

Sunday

Dear Diary,

I know you're dying to find out what happened yesterday. I would have told you last night, except I was totally wiped out after our big rescue mission. Being a hero is hard work!

So here's the scoop, Diary. (I'm writing this while I chow down on a bowl of papaya-kiwi oatmeal, so bear with me.)

Four of us went out in canoes to look for Mary-Kate and Phoebe. Sid and I were in one canoe. Jenny and Brad, two of the camp counsellors, were in the second canoe.

We paddled through the swamp for a really long time. There was no sign of my sister or Phoebe anywhere.

"Mary-Kate! Phoebe! Where are you?" I shouted their names over and over again until my voice was croaky.

But they didn't answer. The only sounds we heard were birds squawking and bullfrogs twanging.

The sky was getting darker, even though it was

the middle of the afternoon. "Looks like it might storm," Brad called out from the other canoe.

"Doesn't look good," Sid agreed.

After a while, we went around a bend in the channel and came to a sort of fork. We paddled to the left, following the little red flags. But then I noticed something.

"Sid? See those spiders' webs up there?" I said.

"Uh-huh. Just keep your head down, they won't bother you," Sid replied. "All the canoes went under them this afternoon."

"So did I," I said. "But Mary-Kate *hates* spiders, and so does Phoebe. There's no way *they* would have gone that way!"

Sid stopped paddling. "Wait up!" he called out to Jenny and Brad. "You mean, you think they would have taken the *right* fork? Even though the red flags point to the left?" he asked me.

"Uh-huh." I pointed my paddle at the narrow channel to the right. "I bet you anything they went that way – and got lost!"

So we all backed up and took the right fork. The channel was skinnier in that direction. There were mangrove roots all over the place, sticking out of the water like black claws.

All of a sudden I noticed a family of alligators

hanging out on the banks of an island. "S-Sid?" I squeaked.

"Let's just keep paddling, okay?" he said in a tense voice.

"No problem!" I got down on my knees and started paddling extra-fast, as if I were in the Canoe Olympics or something. "Mary-Kate! Phoebe! Where are you guys!" I yelled hoarsely.

From far away I heard a voice reply.

"Sid, stop paddling!" I demanded.

Sid put his paddle down. So did Jenny and Brad. Everyone listened intently.

We all heard it then. *"Ashley! Hellllpp!"*

"That's my sister!" I cried out. "Mary-Kate! Phoebe! Hang on, we're coming for you!"

"We're over here! Hellllpp!"

The four of us paddled like crazy, following the sound of Mary-Kate's voice. We paddled and paddled until we reached this mossy little island.

All of a sudden there was a flash of lightning, then a crack of thunder. Just as the sky lit up, I saw Mary-Kate and Phoebe. They were on the banks of the island, jumping up and down and waving their arms.

I leaped out of the canoe and ran across the mangroves. "I thought you guys had got eaten by alligators!" I sobbed as I hugged Mary-Kate.

"I thought you guys *were* alligators when I heard your canoe."

Phoebe wrapped her arms around both of us. "I'm so glad you found us. I guess I won't have to leave you my vintage black dresses, after all!"

I stared at her. "Huh?"

"That's not important any more," Mary-Kate said. "I'm just so glad you found us!"

And I had my sister and my friend back, safe and sound!

Dear Diary,

Life sure seems different when you've had a near-death experience! Now that I've survived alligators, crocodiles, panthers, and near-starvation, I really appreciate the little things more. Like hot oatmeal for breakfast. Like having a real bed to sleep in. Like hanging out with my friends.

Like having the best twin sister in the whole world!

Two for the Road

Ashley and I are speaking to each other again – isn't that great, Diary? After the big rescue yesterday, we all canoed like mad back to Camp Coral Reef. Which was a good thing, since as soon as we hit shore, the skies opened up. We're talking thunder, lightning, the works.

It's so weird! I thought Phoebe and I were gone for twelve hours or something. But it turned out it was only five or six hours from the beginning of the canoe race to the time we got back.

Ashley and I rushed back to our room and took long, hot showers. Afterwards, we just hung out in our robes, gave each other pedicures (Tropical Tangerine!), and had a serious heart-to-heart talk.

"I'm sorry I accused you of messing things up with Ross and me," Ashley added. "I know you were only trying to get us back together."

And then it was *my* turn to apologise. I confessed that I *had* been jealous and cranky these last two weeks because Ashley was winning our bet. She was acing our scuba class, while I was making up all kinds of excuses so I could skip class and hole up in my room.

"After calling *you* a wuss, it turned out that *I* was the real wuss," I said sheepishly.

"It doesn't matter now, because in the end, we

15

both got our scuba certificates," Ashley pointed out.

So we hugged each other and swore that we would never, never, *never* let anything come between us again.

So that's the dramatic, nail-biting ending of our Camp Coral Reef vacation. And now we're about to start on Vacation Number Two – in Miami!

Tomorrow morning, bright and early, we're all saying goodbye to Camp Coral Reef and taking a bus to Miami. We're spending two weeks there before going home for the rest of the summer.

And guess what else? Mrs. Clare, our assistant headmistress from White Oak, said that we were going to be doing something really amazing in Miami. She wouldn't give us any details, though. She said she'd tell us tomorrow.

I'll keep you posted, Diary!

Chapter 3

Monday

Dear Diary,
You'll never believe where I am. Miami! In a huge hotel on the beach with two pools and room service and really cute lifeguards.

Mary-Kate and I have a balcony outside our room where we can watch the sun set over the ocean each night. Total bliss.

Camp Coral Reef already seems like it's a million miles away. We said goodbye to Sid and Brad and Jenny and all the counsellors this morning. Then we got on a bus and drove up the Intercoastal Highway to Miami.

On the bus Mrs. Clare made the big announcement about what we were going to be doing there.

"There will be a four-day sports tournament," she explained. "White Oak and Harrington will join together and form a team. You will compete against seven schools from all over the East Coast."

Mary-Kate and I stared at each other. A sports tournament! Luckily, I was in killer shape from my two weeks of canoeing, scuba-diving, and Frisbee-playing at Camp Coral Reef.

"I just found out about the tournament myself,"

Mrs. Clare went on. "I thought it sounded like fun."

Jeremy raised his hand. "What is it, like a triathlon or something?"

Summer frowned. "If it's a try-athlon, does that mean we only have to *try* doing it? Or what?"

"*Tri* means three, Summer. As in three sports," Mrs. Clare replied. "And yes, there actually *will* be three sports. Bicycling, beach volleyball, and water-skiing."

Phoebe raised her hand. "Can we pick which  sport we want to participate in?" she asked, sounding a little nervous. "I mean, I've never even been water-skiing before."

I tried to imagine Phoebe bouncing over the waves in her vintage 1940s bathing suit, which sagged down to her knees. It wasn't easy.

"Different people will participate in different sports," Mrs. Clare said. "But in any case, don't worry if you're not experienced. The emphasis is on team spirit, cooperation, and having fun. The tournament is  going to raise money to save Florida wildlife. For every team that finishes, the sponsors will donate a thousand dollars to the Wildlife Fund."

"Don't *we* get anything for all our hard work?" Jeremy grumbled.

Mrs. Clare grinned. "The team that finishes first will win a special prize," she said. "I'm not sure what it is yet. We'll find out in the next day or two."

Mrs. Clare said that we would get the rest of the scoop when we got to Miami. Everyone on the bus started buzzing excitedly about the tournament. I turned to Ross, who was sitting behind me. "Isn't this awesome?" I said.

I gave him my best Let's Make Up smile and waited for him to smile back. I was hoping that he'd forgiven me by now, especially after I nearly lost my life trying to save Mary-Kate and Phoebe in the swamp. Well, okay, so maybe that's kind of an exaggeration.

But I guess he was still mad, because he just gave me an icy stare.

"Can't talk," he mumbled. "Busy reading."

I peeked over the back of my seat. He was holding a copy of *Florida Dentistry Today* – upside down! He probably grabbed it out of the seat pocket, just to avoid talking to me. Who was he kidding?

19

Well, at least I still had two weeks to get him to forgive me.

Now, if I could only figure out *how*!

Dear Diary,

Okay. Stay calm. Don't panic. Maybe it's not as bad as it seems.

I'm writing this on hotel stationery. Because my real diary is . . . MISS-ING!!!

Let me take a deep breath and start at the beginning.

This morning we all piled on the bus for Miami. I tossed my suitcase in the storage space under the bus along with everyone else's and took a seat next to Ashley. Then I started to rummage through my backpack for my diary.

It wasn't there.

I was pretty annoyed. But I figured I probably left it in my suitcase. No big deal.

But the first thing I did when I got to our hotel room was unpack my suitcase and fish through it.

Still no diary.

It was all I could think about during lunch. Everyone else was by the pool chowing down on shrimp salad sandwiches and gabbing about the

tournament. But I snuck
away so I could come back
to my room and go through
everything again.

Still no diary.

It's the middle of the after-
noon now. Ashley's over on her bed, writing in her
diary. She has this really determined look on her
face, as if she's trying to figure something out.

"Maybe he's at the pool right now," Ashley
murmured.

"Huh?"

"Ross. Maybe he's at the pool. Hey, you want to
go for a swim?" Ashley looked at me hopefully.

"If you're planning to win Ross back, you
probably don't want my help," I told her. "I've been
pretty useless so far."

Ashley said something about wearing her new
red tankini, but I was only half-listening. All I could
think about was my diary.

My eyes zoomed over to Ashley's backpack,
which was lying next to her. Maybe I put my diary
in her backpack by mistake. Should I tell Ashley it's
missing? Or should I just search her backpack when
she isn't looking?

Maybe I shouldn't worry so much. I don't want

Ashley to know I'm totally freaked out. And hey, what could I have written that's so bad?

Ha! A lot.

Let's see. I wrote that Summer needed a dictionary because she's always mixing up words. I also wrote that Cheryl was a terrible cook, and that Elise was as flaky as apple pie. And wasn't there something about how Justin could use a lifetime supply of breath mints?

It's not like I *meant* to write down those mean things. But Phoebe and I thought we were never going to make it back alive!

And I thought being lost in an alligator-filled swamp was bad.

No one can ever find out what I wrote in my diary. If they do, I might as well give up and go back to Chicago – for good. My life at White Oak would be over.

No one would ever talk to me again!

Chapter 4

Tuesday

Dear Diary,

This morning we all went on a boat ride in Biscayne Bay – except for Jeremy, who had a stomach ache from eating  too much Key lime pie last night and had to stay in his hotel room. Jeremy really, *really* likes to eat.

Captain Sal, the captain of the S.S. *Clambake*, gave us a guided tour. He took us past islands with big, fancy mansions on them. And he told us the names of all the exotic-looking birds that we saw: ibiss, snowy egrets, and roseate spoonbills. Wow! Back in Chicago all we ever see are pigeons.

It was a picture-perfect day. The sun was shining. The sky was blue. Palm trees were swaying in the breeze. And I was wearing my cute new sundress with tropical fish all over it.

Ross was standing at the railing, staring out at the water. He looked as if he was deep in thought about something. It was my big chance.

I sauntered over to him. "Hey," I said cheerfully. "Isn't this fun?"

Ross shrugged. "I guess. Sure." He didn't even

bother to turn his head and look at me.

"How's your hotel room?"

"Fine."

"Who did you end up getting for a roommate?"

He mumbled something.

I frowned. "What?"

"Devon Benjamin," he said through clenched teeth.

"Oh."

I could feel my cheeks turning all red. Across the deck Devon was talking to Elise and Cheryl and pointing to some dolphins that were swimming near the boat. They were hanging on to his every word. Elise and Cheryl, that is – not the dolphins.

"Listen, Ross," I pleaded. "Can't we talk about this?"

"Talk about *what*?"

My heart sank. He wasn't going to make this easy for me. I looked around for Mary-Kate, hoping for an encouraging thumbs-up. But she was off in the corner with Phoebe, whispering like mad about something. What was up with that?

"Ross," I said softly. "I don't like Devon. I like *you*. Devon and I were just— "

"Look! That manatee's in trouble!" Devon interrupted my speech.

"Where?" Mrs. Clare cried out. She was holding on to her enormous hat with the plastic fruit on it so it wouldn't blow away in the breeze.

Everyone rushed over to where Devon, Elise, and Cheryl were standing. "See that fishing boat over there?" Devon said, pointing. "There's a manatee caught in its net!"

"That's awful!" Mary-Kate ran over to us.

We learned all about man-atees at Camp Coral Reef. They're these big marine mammals. And when I say big, I mean big – like ten feet long and a thousand pounds.

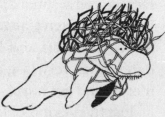

Sid told us that manatees are really cool, gentle animals. They're even vegetarians! The problem is, they're endangered, and they're becoming more endangered all the time.

"Can we help get it loose?" I asked Devon anxiously.

Just as I said that, the manatee wriggled out of the net and swam away all on its own. It was so cute, like an elephant with flippers!

It blinked at us, then disappeared under the water.

"Oh, good, he's all right," Summer said with a

sigh of relief. "It *is* a he, right? What do they call the female ones? Womanatees?"

"They're *all* called manatees," Devon said. "And it may *not* be all right. If it got cut by the net, which can sometimes happen, the cut can get infected. And then the manatee can die from the infection."

"What!" Cheryl exclaimed.

Devon looked pretty upset. "That's part of the reason why manatees are becoming extinct. Fishermen aren't always careful about where they throw their nets and lines into the water. Manatees don't move very fast, and they can get tangled up in them – and get hurt."

Just then I kind of forgot about my problems with Ross. I forgot about everything except for the poor manatee. I really hoped that it was going to be okay.

"Mrs. Clare?" Elise said quietly. "The tournament is going to make lots of money for the Wildlife Fund, right?" I knew just where she was going with that. Elise was a lot like her parents, who were Peace Corps volunteers in Fiji. She was always eager to help others, including animals.

"Right," Mrs. Clare said, nodding. "You're all going to be doing a little something to help save the manatees and other Florida wildlife, too. If you finish, that is."

We are going to finish! I thought. And maybe we'll take first place! After seeing the manatee, I was super-determined to make that happen.

After a while Captain Sal turned the S.S. *Clambake* around and headed back to the marina. As he docked the boat, Mrs. Clare gave us more details about the tournament. We were really pumped up about it.

"There will be a big meeting about the tournament tomorrow morning, with all the other schools in attendance," she explained as we gathered on the dock. "Then, on Thursday morning, we'll have our *own* meeting. At that meeting our team captain will pick who's going to participate in the three different sports." She smiled. "But first you're all going to have to pick a team captain."

Team captain? I thought. That would be me!

Okay, so I'm not all that great at volleyball. But I'm a whiz on a bicycle. And I learned to water-ski on Lake Michigan near Chicago.

But none of that really matters, anyway. What I do best is motivate. Organise. Inspire.

I nudged Mary-Kate. "Nominate me," I whispered.

Mary-Kate seemed startled. She must have been thinking of something else. But just as she began to raise her hand, we heard a familiar voice behind us. Much too familiar.

"Hi, guys," Dana Woletsky called out. "What's up?"

Oh, no! What was *she* doing here?

Heads whipped around. A big white yacht was docking alongside the S.S. *Clambake*. Dana was  standing on deck, wearing a killer blue sundress and supercool-looking shades. Her mom was at the helm, and her dad was tugging on the sails. I recognised them from the times they visited Dana at White Oak.

Dana was a White Oak First Former, too. She and I weren't exactly best buds. It all started when Mary-Kate and I transferred to White Oak from our school in Chicago. I asked Ross to the Sadie Hawkins Dance. Dana accused me of stealing Ross away from her. She had this idea that he was *her* boyfriend. Which was totally not true. But ever since then she's had it in for me.

Dana came down and joined us on the dock. Her mom and dad followed with a couple of Dana's suitcases. Summer ran up and gave Dana a big hug. Ross waved at her.

Two for the Road

Mrs. Clare beamed. "Dana! We're so glad you made it!"

"I didn't know you were going to be on this trip," I blurted out to Dana.

Dana glared at me.

Mrs. Clare smiled and said, "Dana's family arranged to return early from a cruise in the Bahamas so Dana could join us for the Miami leg of the trip," she explained. "And just in time to help us choose a team captain!"

Summer's hand shot up. "I nominate Dana," she said.

"I second her," Ross said.

"What?" I gasped.

"I nominate Ashley," Mary-Kate said quickly.

"I second her," Phoebe said.

I held my breath and waited for Ross to say, "I change my mind, I want *Ashley* to be team captain!" Or something like that. But he didn't say a word.

Oh, Diary! How could Ross side with Dana after all we've been through together? I know he's still angry with me about Devon. But he knows it was just a misunderstanding. Why can't he just get over it?

Anyway, Diary, we're going to vote on team captain tomorrow morning. I've got to get out there and drum up some support. So that means now I have two goals. Beat Dana for team captain. And get Ross back!

Dear Diary,

It's official. I'm definitely doomed.

I've looked everywhere for the diary. I looked through Ashley's backpack, her suitcase, and her dressing table drawers, too. I looked through all my stuff for the sixth time.

There's no sign of it anywhere.

I'm writing this on a pad of hotel stationery. The guy at the front desk must think I have a lot of friends back home, because I keep asking him for more and more stationery.

I'm sitting in the Café Tango, which is a restaurant in the Little Havana section of Miami. Mrs. Clare brought us here for lunch after our boat ride on the S.S. *Clambake*.

Ashley's in a really crabby mood, even though I nominated her for team captain. I think it has something to do with the fact that Dana showed up out of the blue. Plus, Dana is sitting at a table with Summer and Elise – and Ross! Dana's parents were planning on heading off to Key West in their yacht, after they dropped her luggage off at our hotel. Too bad they didn't take Dana with them!

But I can't think about Ashley's problems right now. My problems are *way* bigger. I've hardly touched my black beans and rice and fried plantains because I'm so upset.

I kind of told Phoebe what was going on, during the boat ride, but she didn't seem to care too much.

"If Cheryl or Seth or someone finds your diary and reads our Last Will and Testament, we can just explain that we were temporarily insane," Phoebe said reasonably. "Who could blame us? We were staring death right in the face!"

Let's just say we agreed to disagree on this. After all, it's *my* diary. It's *my* handwriting. If anyone's going to take the fall for this, it's me!

I know, I know! There's a chance I dropped the diary on the beach by accident, and it's sinking to the bottom of the Atlantic Ocean as we speak. If I'm lucky.

But if I'm *not* so lucky, and one of my friends *does* have it, I have to get it back – pronto!

Chapter 5

Wednesday

Dear Diary,

This morning we had the big meeting for the sports tournament. Angela Velasquez, the sports director of the hotel, told us the deal while about a hundred of us munched down on bagels and cream cheese and guava smoothies on the beach.

"There are eight schools here from the East Coast that will be competing," she said. "Each school is responsible for choosing its own team captain by noon today."

Dana and I exchanged a glance. She flipped her hair over her shoulders and gave me a smug look, like she knew exactly who *our* team captain was going to be. We'd see about that!

Yesterday afternoon I bought a dozen big cookies at the bakery across the street from the hotel. I

bought a tube of blue icing, too, and wrote "Ashley for team captain!" on the cookies. I gave one to everyone in our group after dinner, along with a flyer that listed all the reasons why I would make a good team captain.

Like:
- PROVEN LEADERSHIP QUALITIES!
- MOTIVATED TO WIN!
- DEDICATED TO THE CAUSE OF WILDLIFE!
- WILL WORK OVERTIME FOR YOU!

Everyone seemed pretty impressed by the cookies and flyers. Except for Summer, who is way too loyal to Dana. And Ross, who threw his cookie and flyer in the trash. Hmmm.

Angela held her clipboard in the air. "As you all know, the tournament will consist of three sports. Volleyball, water-skiing, and bicycling. We start on Sunday with round-robin volleyball. Monday will be the elimination volleyball event. Tuesday will be water-skiing. And we'll finish up on Wednesday with a 10K bike race."

Some guy in the back row stood up and raised his hand. I practically choked on my bagel. He was really super-cut, and he wore a T-shirt that said NO PAIN, NO GAIN. He looked as if he could bench-press two hundred pounds in his sleep.

No pain, no gain

In fact, a lot of the guys and girls in the crowd looked like pretty serious athletes. We – White Oak and Harrington – were in for some major competition!

"Does everyone compete in all three sports?" Mr. No Pain, No Gain asked Angela.

"No," Angela replied. She glanced quickly at her clipboard. "There are ten to twelve of you per school. Each school should have a maximum of six people competing in each sport. So it's up to the team captains to decide which six people will compete in each of the three sports."

Phoebe leaned over to me and whispered, "Do I really *have* to participate? Can't I just write about this for the *Acorn*?" She was the editor of the White Oak First Form newspaper and was always looking for stuff to write about.

"Mrs. Clare says we *all* have to participate in at least one of the events. *And* finish. Or the money doesn't go to the Wildlife Fund," I whispered back. "Don't worry, Phoebe. We'll get you a pair of spandex bike shorts with racing stripes. Vintage 1980s. It'll help you get into the spirit of things!"

"The team captains will have the next few days to decide who competes in which sport and to lead the practises for those sports." Angela grinned. "I'm sure your school chaperons have told you that the tournament's sponsors will donate one thousand dollars to the Wildlife Fund for every team that finishes. That means that if every team finishes, eight thousand dollars will go towards helping to save Florida wildlife!"

Everyone cheered. I raised my fist in the air and cheered, too.

"And there's more," Angela added. "Whichever school finishes first will get a special grand prize."

I held my breath. I wondered what it would be.

"The first-place school," Angela went on, "will win a trip to Seaquarium, where you'll get to name their brand-new baby manatee – plus swim with the dolphins!"

A baby manatee! Swimming with the dolphins! I couldn't believe it. Now I really, really, *really* wanted our team to win.

And I was just the person to lead us to victory!

After the big meeting was over, Mrs. Clare called our group aside. "Okay, gang. We have two nominations for team captain on the table. Let's take a vote."

Gulp! I glanced around. I knew Phoebe and Mary-Kate would vote for me. I knew Summer and Ross would vote for Dana, unless Ross had come to his senses and forgiven me.

I had no idea how Jeremy, Justin, Seth, Devon,

Elise, and Cheryl would vote, though. And what if it was a tie? *Then* what?

The big moment came. "All those for Dana Woletsky?" Mrs. Clare said.

A bunch of hands shot up. Summer, Ross, Elise, Seth, and Dana.

"You can't vote for yourself, Dana," Mrs. Clare told her. "Okay, that's four votes for Dana. All those for Ashley Burke?"

Phoebe, Mary-Kate, Jeremy, Justin, Devon, and Cheryl raised their hands.

Mrs. Clare smiled. "We have a winner! Ashley Burke will be our team captain!"

YESSSSSS!!!! It was all I could do to keep from jumping up and down and screaming for joy.

Team Captain!

Mary-Kate high-fived me. "Way to go, sis!"

"Congratulations, Ashley!" Phoebe said, hugging me. "I can't wait to profile you for the *Acorn*."

Jeremy slapped me on the back. Hard. "I only voted for you because of the cookie."

"Thanks, Jeremy, I appreciate that," I said sweetly.

At that moment I would have been in a really good mood except for two things. (Well, three things, if you include Jeremy's comment.)

First, Ross didn't say a word to me. No "Congratulations." No "Good luck." No nothing.

And second, Dana *did* say a word to me. A bunch of words, in fact. And they sent a chill up my spine.

"If you think this team's going to finish, you are so wrong," she said. "Just you wait!"

What did she mean by that?

Dear Diary,

After lunch, while we were all hanging out at the pool, I told Ashley about the missing diary.

"What if someone has it?" I said miserably. "There are a *lot* of things in there that I wouldn't want anyone to read!"

But Ashley didn't seem too concerned.

"You probably dropped it somewhere back at Camp Coral Reefs," Ashley shrugged. "Some alligators probably chowed down on it. I wouldn't worry about it if I were you. I wonder if *this* would be a good practise schedule. . ." She nibbled on her pencil, then hunched over her clipboard and began scribbling like mad.

Okay, well, so much for sympathy. Phoebe wasn't worried, either. She was sitting in a lounge chair, wearing these huge bug-like sunglasses and reading a novel about Florida in the 1930s. Even when I reminded her about all the horrible things I wrote, she just told me again not to freak out about it.

Just then, I heard a noise in the bushes behind us. "What was that?" I said, turning around.

"Hmm?" Phoebe wasn't even paying attention. "What was *what*?"

I looked and looked, but I didn't see anything – or anyone – in the bushes. I guess I was just imagining things.

I peeked over the top of my shades and did a

quick sweep of the pool area. Ross, Seth, and Justin were having a cannonball competition in the deep end. Devon was demonstrating jackknife dives for Elise and Cheryl off the diving board. Dana and Summer were sipping iced tea and flipping through a stack of fashion magazines.

So far no one had come up to me and said anything about my diary. Maybe Ashley and Phoebe were right. Maybe I did drop it in the swamp. Because if someone had it, we would have heard about it by now.

But maybe they were wrong. Maybe the person who had it was just lying low. Biding time, trying to figure out the best time to attack.

This was driving me crazy. I couldn't just wait around for someone to get even with me. But what could I do?

Chapter 6

Thursday

Dear Diary,

Okay, so I came up with this brilliant plan to figure out who has my diary. *If* anyone has it, that is.

I figured that whoever has it would have read everything in it.

So I decided to go down the list of suspects, one by one, and ask each person a bunch of really sneaky, subtle questions. That way I could figure out if the person had read my diary or not.

I started with Cheryl. At breakfast I found her sitting alone on the terrace. She was writing postcards and picking at a bowl of oatmeal.

"Hey, Cheryl!" I pulled up a chair and sat down next to her.

"Hey, Mary-Kate."

"Writing some postcards?"

"Yeah, to my parents and my grandparents and my aunt Sally in Connecticut."

I nodded and smiled. I tried to remember what I had written in the Last Will and Testament about Cheryl. And then it came to me. *To Cheryl Miller, a copy of* Cooking 101 for Dummies, *because her brownies taste like baked swamp slime. . .*

I wondered how I was going to steer the conversation around to the subject of cooking. And then I noticed that Cheryl had cutely arranged the blueberries on the oatmeal so that they formed a smiley face. I saw my opportunity.

"That is so *cute!*" I gushed. "You have such a way with food!"

Cheryl gave me a funny look. "Uh, I just moved a few blueberries around. It's no big deal."

I laughed nervously. "Oh, but it's not just the blueberries! You are such an awesome cook!"

"I am?" Cheryl looked surprised.

I nodded. "You are! I remember those . . . those . . . *brownies* you made that time, for Elise's birthday. They were amazing!"

"They were?" Cheryl beamed.

"Did you get the recipe from a cookbook? You must use cookbooks, right?" I was really homing in on the dirt now.

Cheryl smiled and shrugged. "Not really. I kind of just eyeball everything. You know, a cup of this, a teaspoon of that, pop it in the oven, see what happens."

"How about that new cookbook? I thought you

might have it. *Cooking 101 for Dummies*?"

Cheryl's smile disappeared. *"Cooking 101 for DUMMIES*? Are you saying I'm a *dummy*?"

Oh, no! I realised that my sneaky, subtle interrogation had just taken a nosedive. "No, no, that's not what I meant! What I meant was—"

But it was too late. Cheryl picked up her bowl of oatmeal and her postcards and rose to her feet. "I think I'll eat *inside*," she snapped.

Oops!

I guess I'm not as sneaky and subtle as I thought.

The good news is, it doesn't seem like Cheryl has my diary. One down, eight to go!

Dear Diary,

We had our team tryouts this morning after breakfast. I'd spent all yesterday afternoon and evening preparing for it, so I was ready. Raring to go, in fact.

"Okay, listen up!" I said loudly.

Everyone was gathered around the volleyball net. I was dressed in my new white SAVE THE MANATEES tank top, matching shorts, and visor, and I had a whistle around my neck. I looked *so* official.

"This morning I'm going to hold tryouts for the

three different sports," I explained. "Then tomorrow morning I'll announce who's going to be on which team."

Dana raised her hand. "You're going to pick me for the water-skiing team, right?" she said sweetly.

"You've got to try out, just like everyone else," I told her. Dana glared at me. "Any other questions before we get started?"

Summer fluttered her nails in the air. "I just had a manicure, so I really can't play volleyball. Could you pick me for one of the other sports?"

I sighed. Being a team captain wasn't easy. "Sorry, Summer, everyone has to try out for all three sports."

Jeremy raised his hand. "Hey, boss? How many hours a day are you going to make us practise?"

"Just in the mornings. In the afternoons we're all free to do whatever we want. We'll have practices tomorrow and Saturday. The tournament begins on Sunday."

After a few more questions we finally got started. I had everyone try out for volleyball, then water-skiing, then bicycling. Angela Velasquez had organised things so each school had the time, space, and equipment necessary to hold the tryouts.

By the end of the morning I was covered with sand and sweat – and my clipboard was covered with notes. I had all three teams picked out – almost.

There was just one problem. Her name was Dana!

You'll never believe what she did during the try-outs, Diary. She wanted to be on the water-skiing team so badly that she actually *faked* being bad at volleyball and bicycling. I could tell she was faking – it was totally obvious. Plus, I knew from White Oak that she was good at those two sports.

The thing was, she wasn't good at water-skiing. She wasn't faking *that*. I was way better than she was. And I really wanted Devon and Cheryl on the water-skiing team, and Mary-Kate, Summer, and Jeremy, too.

That meant that I had to decide between Dana and me for the last spot on the water-skiing team. No one else even knew how to water-ski.

What was I going to do?

Chapter 7

Friday

Dear Diary,

Yesterday afternoon, after the try-outs, a bunch of us decided to go Rollerblading in South Miami Beach. Or SoBe, as it's known to the locals.

It was totally cool! There was a long boardwalk for Rollerblading that ran along the beach and Ocean Drive. It was lined with palm trees and tropical-looking flowers. Most of the women Rollerbladers we saw were wearing itty-bitty bikinis, and most of the guys were wearing Speedos. Holy cow!

Phoebe was checking out something else altogether. "Look at the amazing Art Deco architecture!" she cried out.

She pointed to the hotels and restaurants on Ocean Drive. I had never seen buildings that looked like that. There were pink buildings and baby-blue buildings and yellow buildings. A lot of them had chrome trim, old-fashioned neon signs, and pictures of flamingos on them.

"I feel like we're back in the 1930s!" Phoebe sighed happily.

I wonder if the people in the 1930s wore bikinis and Speedos? I didn't think so!

I noticed that Ross was Rollerblading at the back, by himself. Ashley had stayed at the hotel, to do some serious brainstorming about who to pick for her three teams. I decided to take the opportunity to interrogate him. Maybe *he* had my diary?

I tried to remember what I had written in the Last Will and Testament about him. Oh, yeah.

To Ross Lambert, a dartboard with a picture of Devon Benjamin on it . . .

I dug in my stopper and waited until Ross had caught up. "Hey, Ross," I said with a smile.

"Oh, hi, Mary-Kate," he said. He didn't look totally thrilled to see me. "What's up?"

"Isn't this a blast?" I said cheerfully.

"Uh-huh."

"We should really get them to put in a Rollerblading path between White Oak and Harrington. Don't you think so?"

"Sure. I guess." He adjusted his helmet and gazed off in the distance, at a motorboat gunning through the water.

Okay, just go for it, I told myself. "So! What else do you like to do in your spare time, besides Rollerblade? Do you have any hobbies?"

"Huh?" Ross stared at me. "Do I have any *hobbies*?"

"You know, like, stamp collecting, or piano playing, or bird-watching. Or what about darts? Do you like to play darts? Do you have a dartboard at home?"

"Uh, yeah, I have a dartboard." Ross was looking at me as if I were crazy. "I got one for Christmas last year."

"Really? Do you ever . . . ha ha . . . put a picture of anyone up on it? You know, like if you're mad at them or something?"

"A picture of . . . " Ross's eyes suddenly flashed. "Sure! Your sister gave me her school picture last fall. I think I know just what to do with it now! Thanks for the idea!" And with  that he sped up until he was Rollerblading alongside Summer and Dana.

Great. Just what the Burke sisters needed – more bad PR with Ross Lambert!

But I wasn't going to be a quitter. I tried my sneaky, subtle approach two more times – with Seth and Elise.

I ended up putting my foot in my mouth with them, too! By the end of the day, I decided.

No more interrogations!

Dear Diary,

This morning I gathered the troops together on the beach and announced who was going to be on which team.

"The volleyball team will be Dana, Justin, Summer, Ross, Jeremy, and Mary-Kate," I said, reading off my clipboard.

Summer glanced at her nails. "I hope they're dry by now!"

"The bicycling team will be Phoebe, Ross, Dana, Elise, Seth, and me," I went on. I *had* to pick Phoebe, since that was the only sport she was willing to do. Ross was the best cyclist. Elise was the worst. But Elise had to be on the team, because she couldn't do the other two sports at all.

"Excellent!" Seth said. He and Ross exchanged high fives.

I took a deep breath. I noticed that Dana's eyes were boring holes into me.

"The water-skiing team will be . . ." I took another deep breath. "Devon, Cheryl, Mary-Kate, Summer, Jeremy. And me."

"*What!*"

That came from Dana. "Why aren't I on the

water-skiing team?" she shrieked.

"I'm sorry, Dana. We can talk about this later."

Dana put her hands on her hips. "We can talk about it *now*! I demand an explanation!"

"Dana, not now." I tried to sound in charge. "Okay, everybody! The tournament starts in two days. We've got a lot to do. Here's how the practices are going to go. . . ."

Dana looked at me with pure fury. Then she leaned over and whispered something to Summer. Summer started giggling.

I raised my voice and tried to sound even more assertive. "I'm going to divide you all into your teams . . ."

I sent the bicycling team off, minus me, to do laps around the neighbourhood. I put Mary-Kate in charge of the volleyball team, to work on serves. I asked Devon to oversee the water-skiing team, to practise jumps. I had scheduled everything down to the last minute, so that the people who were on more than one team could split their time between sports.

We all worked hard for the next few hours. The sun was beating down, and the sand felt as though it had been baked. Clutching my clipboard, I went from team to team. I supervised, observed, took notes, and made suggestions for improvements.

When I got to the volleyball team, Mary-Kate called me aside. Everyone was taking a five-minute break to pour the contents of their water bottles over their heads.

"Dana's messing things up," she whispered. "Every time she gets the ball, she knocks it out of bounds. It's taking forever just to let everyone serve!"

I stared at Dana. She took a long swig from her water bottle, then stared at me.

"Is there a problem here, Dana?" I asked her.

Dana flipped her hair over her shoulders. "Problem? There's no problem!"

Ross walked up to Dana and tapped her on the shoulder. "You're not getting a good angle on the ball. Here, let me show you what I do. . ."

Dana slipped her hand through his arm. "Oh, that is so sweet, Ross, would you?" She gave me a mean smile.

Oh, Diary! Why did Dana have to show up in Miami????

Dear Diary,
    Things are bad. Really, really, *really* bad.

Two for the Road

Maybe I should pack my bags right now and fly back to Chicago and go into hiding – forever!

It turns out that someone has my diary, after all.

This afternoon, after practice, I went up to my hotel room to take a shower. There was an envelope under the door, addressed to me.

There was a note in it. The letters in the message had been cut out of a magazine and glued onto the paper. It said:

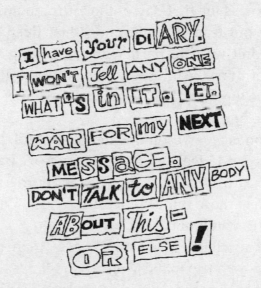

Chapter 8

Saturday

Dear Diary,

We had practice again this morning, and it went pretty well. Except that Dana didn't show up. She said she had a headache and had to stay in her room. And Mary-Kate was acting kind of distracted during her water-skiing runs. I wonder what's up with her? Tomorrow is the first day of the tournament! I really feel like our team is coming together. Even Phoebe, who didn't want to participate, is getting into the swing of things. And Elise, who's the weak link on the bicycling team, has been working super-hard to improve her times.

Devon is an awesome water-skier. Still, I look at him now and I feel – nothing. No sweaty palms, no racing heart. What did I ever see in him?

I *do* feel those things when I see Ross. Will I ever be able to win him back, Diary?

I had my chance after practice. Mrs. Clare rounded us all up for a trip to the Monkey Jungle.

The Monkey Jungle is kind of a zoo just for monkeys, gorillas, orangutans, gibbons, and other primates. The *really* cool thing is, the humans have to be in cages while the animals run around free!

I went up to Ross, who was checking out a bunch of macaques chasing one another up a palm tree. "Hey, Ross."

"Hey, Ashley," he said. Well, he was talking to me, anyway. There was hope!

"Those monkeys are pretty funny," I remarked.

"Yeah." There was a silence, then he added, "I really hope we win first place."

I smiled. "Yeah, me, too."

He started to say something else. But just then Dana came sauntering up to us. I guess she was feeling all better from her headache.

"Hey, Ross!" she said, giving him a big smile. She looped her arm through his. "Come here, I want to show you something!"

"Um, just a moment, I was in the middle of—"

"Come on, it'll just take a sec!" Dana brushed up really close to him and gave him another big smile.

Ross gave me an apologetic look, then the two of them went off. Ross said something to her, and she threw her head back and laughed.

Grrr!

Does Dana like Ross? Or is she just trying to

make me really, really upset? Because I have to tell you, Diary, it's working!

Dear Diary,

I hardly slept a wink last night because I was tossing and turning about the anonymous note. I kept thinking about it all during practice, and while we were at the Monkey Jungle, too.

One of my friends has my diary. He or she could start blabbing about what I wrote any second. Then everyone will hate me forever. How awful is *that*?

Tonight, we had a pizza party on the beach. The sun was setting over the water and turning it reddish-gold. I hardly touched my conch and pineapple slice.

Everyone was buzzing about the tournament.

"The round-robin volleyball event is first," Ashley explained as she chowed down on a slice of shrimp and mango pizza. "That means the eight teams are divided into two sections."

Summer blinked. "Are there birds involved? Why is it called round-robin?"

"It's *round* because we go around and around until we've played everyone in our section,"

Ashley replied. "I don't know about the *robin* part. Maybe some guy named Robin invented the idea."

"Did Batman help?" Jeremy cracked up at his own joke.

"Ha-ha," Elise said.

While everyone talked, I glanced around the circle. I kept wondering who had my diary. Dana? No. She didn't join the group till late. Cheryl? Jeremy? Elise? Summer? Seth? Justin?

The person had written "Wait for my next message." When would that be happening? And what would the message say?

After dinner a bunch of people went off for a dip in the pool. Ashley wanted to take a walk on the beach and do some last-minute strategising for tomorrow.

I decided to go up to my room and sulk.

I grabbed a bunch of magazines and lay down on my bed. A balmy breeze blew through my window and stirred the curtains around. I could see a thin little sliver of a crescent moon in the sky.

I was just getting started on an article called "Do You Know Who Your Friends *Really* Are?" when I heard the sound of footsteps at my door. Quiet footsteps, as if the person didn't want to be heard.

I sat up, my heart hammering in my chest. I saw

a white envelope being slipped under the door.

I jumped out of bed and ran to the door – and flung it open.

"Ow!"

The diary thief was standing there, rubbing his head from where I'd banged him with the door-knob.

It was Jeremy!

I grabbed the envelope and ripped it open. Inside, there was a note like the one I got yesterday, with the letters cut out from a magazine. The note said:

"You have my diary!" I cried out.

Jeremy glanced around. "Shhhh!" he hissed.

He grabbed my arm and pushed me into my room, then he closed the door. "Quiet! Someone might hear us!" he snapped.

hear us!" he snapped.

"Jeremy, how could you?" I said angrily. "You

have to give me back my diary right now!"

"Not so fast," he said with a sly smile. "First, you have to do me some favours."

I didn't like the sound of that. "Favours? What favours?"

"First, the doughnuts. After that . . . I'll let you know."

I glared at him. "And what if I refuse?"

"Then I'm going to tell Cheryl and Ross and Seth, and everyone else what you wrote about them," Jeremy warned. "Let's see. What was my favourite? Something about *GuyStyle* magazine?"

He really *did* have my diary. Jeremy, who put a goldfish in my sippy cup when we were three. Jeremy, who taped a "Kick Me" sign on the back of my homecoming dress.

I was doomed!

"Oh, all right," I said through clenched teeth. "I'll do whatever you say."

Jeremy looked smug. "Good. We have a deal."

Could I trust him? Totally not. He could make me do all these favours and still blab about my diary to everyone.

On the other hand, did I have a choice?

Chapter 9

Sunday

Dear Diary,

The tournament is underway!

It kicked off this morning. I went down to the beach after breakfast with everyone else. Four volleyball nets had been set up. There were dozens of kids scattered around, doing warm-up stretches and laps.

Angela Velasquez got up on a little stage and held up a megaphone. "Welcome, everyone! We're about to start the round-robin competition."

"Go, Oakdale!" someone shouted.

"Okay, here's the deal," Angela went on. "The eight schools are divided into two sections. Your team captains have the section assignments. If you're in Section One, you have to play the other three teams in your section. At the end of the day we'll tally who's won the most games. May the best team win!"

The crowd cheered. I gathered my volleyball team together, and we went into a huddle. "Our first game is against Teasdale Junior High, from Maryland," I said, reading off the sheet Angela had given me. "We can beat them! Think positive! Remember why we're doing this!"

"To score free tickets to Seaquarium?" Jeremy piped up.

"To help save Florida wildlife," I corrected him. "Watch out for the tall redheaded girl with the killer serve. I saw her during practice yesterday, and she's really good. Justin, take it easy with the spikes. Dana, remember to keep your eye on the ball. Okay, good luck, everyone!"

We burst out of the huddle with a big cheer and trotted over to the volleyball net. The Teasdale team was waiting for us. They looked . . . *determined*. Well, so were we!

I took a deep breath and watched from the side-lines as my team members took their places. Angela blew the whistle to start the game.

"Go, team!" I said, pumping my fist in the air. "You can do it!"

That first game was a nail-biter. The tall red-headed girl from Teasdale really *did* have a killer serve. No one on our team could come close to it.

But we ended up winning that game, anyway. Ross, Summer, and Justin were in top form. Mary-Kate seemed a little distracted, but she played really well, too. Jeremy pulled his weight.

And best of all, Dana was on good behaviour. She didn't mess up shots or anything like that.

We lost the next game, against Immaculate Heart from Delaware – by a hair.

By the end of the day, we were ranked third among the nine teams. I asked Angela what that meant for the rest of the tournament.

"That means that for you to come in first place overall, you have to win the next two out of three events: the elimination volleyball competition tomorrow, water-skiing on Tuesday, or the bicycle race on Wednesday," she explained.

Two out of three? Hey, no problem!

I was beginning to think that we really *could* win the gold.

Dear Diary,

The nightmare has begun.

Okay, so it's great that we did so well in the round-robin competition today. But how can you enjoy the thrill of victory when your life is being ruined by a black-mailing rat . . . named Jeremy Burke?

I quickly found out what he meant by "favours." He wanted me to be his personal maid.

After the volleyball competition, he told me to

fetch him a towel. And a glass of iced tea. And then a special squiggly straw for the iced tea.

He got even more carried away at dinner time. Mrs. Clare had organised a big clambake at Egret Point, down the beach from the hotel. During the clambake, Jeremy kept ordering me around: "Get me seconds, Mary-Kate." "I need another drink, Mary-Kate." "You didn't put enough butter on the corn, Mary-Kate."

Ashley was hanging out with Phoebe. At one point she noticed that I was carrying a plate of clams and potato salad over to Jeremy. She made a beeline in my direction and tapped me on the shoulder.

"Okay, I'm a little confused," Ashley said. "Why are you bringing Jeremy his food?"

"I'm just trying to be nice," I lied. "He's our cousin – a family member. What's the big deal?"

"Nice to *Jeremy*?" Ashley said incredulously. "Don't you remember the time he filled your shampoo bottle with maple syrup? Or when he sent you anonymous letters saying that you had bad breath?"

I clamped my hand over my mouth. "Is my breath okay?"

"You do *not* have bad breath," Ashley said

impatiently. "That's not the point. The point is, Jeremy has been harassing you – and me – since we were born. So why are you being nice to him?"

I shrugged.

Ashley narrowed her eyes at me. "Are you feeling okay? What is it, are you still stressed out about your missing diary?"

I grabbed her arm. "Shhh!" I hissed. "Don't even mention that!" I glanced over at Jeremy to make sure he hadn't overheard. He had said in his first note that I wasn't supposed to talk to anyone about the diary.

But he didn't seem to be paying attention. He was too busy chowing down on his clams.

He noticed me looking at him. "Yo, Mary-Kate!" he called out. Although it was hard to understand him because his mouth was full of clams. "Hurry up with that plate! And where's my lemonade? Did you forget my lemonade?"

"Oh, sorry, Jeremy, I'll be right back with that!" I replied sweetly. Was there some way I could slip a bad clam onto his plate? I wondered.

"I only have three words to say to you," Ashley said. "Are . . . you . . . nuts?"

"Just trust me," I said with a sigh. "I know what I'm doing."

Bad Clam

Chapter 10

Monday

Dear Diary,

After dinner last night Jeremy made me hand-wash his lucky socks so they would be dry in time for the elimination volleyball competition today. Then this morning he called me at the crack of dawn.

"Rise and shine!" he said when I'd picked up the phone.

"What *time* is it?" I mumbled. Across the room Ashley groaned and hid her head under the covers.

"It's time to get me breakfast," Jeremy said cheerfully. "Call room service for me, would you, M.K.? Let's see, how about three poached eggs, a side of bacon, a side of ham, a side of sausage, and a yogurt smoothie? I gotta be in top form for the volleyball competition today, so I need a lot of protein."

"Hang on." I reached over to the nightstand for a piece of paper and a pen. "You could have called room service yourself," I muttered as I scribbled his order.

"What was that, M.K.? I didn't hear you."

"Nothing."

"Oh, and hey, where are my lucky socks?"

"They're almost dry," I snapped. "Can I go now?"

"Yeah. Except, try to work on your attitude, okay? You're kind of crabby today. I don't like crabby."

"I'll work on it," I snapped, and slammed down the phone.

Ashley's head popped out from under the covers. "Who was *that*?"

"Oh, nobody. Wrong number."

Ashley glared at me suspiciously. "I'm going back to sleep now. Try not to get any more wrong numbers, okay?"

 I dragged the phone into the bathroom and called room service from there, so Ashley wouldn't hear. Jeremy's lucky socks were hanging on the shower rack. I forced myself to touch them. They were dry.

Oh, Diary – what has my life come to? Maybe I should just call Jeremy's bluff and let him blab about my Last Will and Testament. Could losing all my friends be any worse than being his slave twenty-four hours a day?

Then I thought about the mean things I'd written about Cheryl and Summer and everyone else.

I realised that there was no way around it. I needed Jeremy to keep my secret . . . a secret.

I thought Jeremy might leave me alone until

lunch time, but I was wrong. He had plans for me during the elimination volleyball competition.

The competition started at nine o'clock sharp. The deal was this: the top four teams from yesterday's round-robin competition would participate.

Since we came in third place yesterday, we were up. In the semi-final round, we were playing Oakdale Middle School from North Carolina. If we won that round, we would be in the finals. And if we won that, we would be the winners.

"Yo, M.K.," Jeremy called out just before we were ready to start playing Oakdale. "I need you to do me a favour."

I gritted my teeth. "What?"

"Whenever you get the ball, pass it to me, okay?" he whispered, glancing around. "I want to get lots of shots over the net."

"No way!" I cried out. "Ashley'll have a fit!"

Jeremy narrowed his eyes at me. "Okay, then. Let's see, where's Summer? I'm sure she'd be *real* interested in knowing what you left her in your will. And what about—"

"All right, all right." I glared at him. "I'll pass you the ball."

Two of a Kind Diaries

Dear Diary,

Has my sister totally lost her mind?
During the game against Oakdale
this morning, she kept passing the ball
to Jeremy. Then *he* would get the point.

And every time Jeremy made a point, he would

do this obnoxious little dance and
shout, "I rule, you drool!" to the
Oakdale players. That was typical
Jeremy. But Mary-Kate wasn't acting like typical Mary-Kate.

I called her aside during a break.
"Okay, what's up?" I snapped.

"What do you mean?" Mary-Kate said innocently.

"Why do you keep passing the ball to Cousin
Dearest?"

"I'm trying to set up shots for my fellow team
members instead of hogging the ball," she
explained reasonably.

"Your fellow team members? You're not passing
the ball to anyone but Jeremy!"

"But we're winning, aren't we?" Mary-Kate
pointed out defensively.

"Just pass the ball to someone else from now on,
okay?" I said. "Or hit it over the net yourself. That's
an order!"

Was it my imagination, or did Mary-Kate look really panic-stricken when I said that? She rushed over to Jeremy and whispered something to him. What was going on between those two?

In the end we managed to win the semi-final round against Oakdale. We were in the finals!

We had to play a really tough-looking school from Connecticut, Coate Academy. Everyone on their team was super-cut and six feet tall, even the girls. Because it was the finals, all the other schools gathered around to watch. Talk about pressure!

The score was practically tied the whole game. There was just one problem. This time it wasn't Jeremy. It was Dana who kept jumping in front of everyone else to get the ball.

I called a quick time-out and went up to Dana. "Dana," I whispered. "I really appreciate how hard you're playing. But you've got to stay in your spot and let other people have the ball once in a while."

Dana flipped her hair over her shoulders. "Why?"

"Because this is a team," I reminded her. "You've got to let your teammates get the ball sometimes."

Dana glared at me. "Whatever."

The game resumed. It was down to a single point. If Coate won the next point, they were going to win the game – and the event. We had to hold the line.

It was Coate's serve. When the serve came, Ross fell to his knees and bobbed it over to Jeremy, who slammed it over the net. A guy on the Coate team returned it. He hadn't got a good angle on it, though, so it came back over the net at a slow, steady speed. It would be an easy shot for us.

The ball came towards Dana. All she had to do was move a little to the left. No problem, I thought.

But Dana didn't move. Not an inch. The ball fell to the ground and rolled around and around in the sand.

"We win!" someone on the Coate team shouted. "We win the competition!" The crowd broke into wild applause.

Dana turned around and looked right at me. "You told me to stay in my spot," she said with a shrug.

I realised what had happened.

She had missed the shot deliberately.

Chapter 11

Monday

Dear Diary,

I know I already wrote to you today, Diary. But I had to write to you again.

Because I am having a really, really, *really* bad day!

At dinner time I was still miffed about Dana missing that shot. I knew she did it on purpose, just to make me mad!

Well, it worked!

I decided I wasn't going to say anything to Dana about any of this. Not a word. I mean, why let her know that I care?

But then Dana came sauntering up to my table during dinner. I was sitting with Mary-Kate and Phoebe, munching down on hot dogs and spicy coleslaw.

"Hi, guys," Dana said cheerfully. She looked even more smug than usual. "Great game today, Mary-Kate. Too bad we lost!"

"Well, it was close, anyway," Mary-Kate said distractedly. She tried to squirt mustard on her hot dog and missed.

"Tomorrow *is* another day," Phoebe piped up.

"Maybe you should work on your defence, Mary-Kate," Dana suggested. "We probably would have won if you hadn't passed all those shots to Jeremy."

Mary-Kate gasped. I felt blood rushing to my cheeks. "*What*?" I cried out. "We lost because of *you*, Dana. We would have won if you hadn't missed that piece-of-cake shot in the end. On purpose!"

Dana laughed. "I did no such thing. You're the one who told me to stay in my spot!"

"That's not what I meant, and you know it!" I snapped. "Everyone saw you miss that shot. And everyone knows why you did it, too. You've been after me ever since I got voted team captain instead of you! You're just jealous!" I was so angry, my voice squeaked on those last few words.

As luck would have it, Ross had overheard this entire conversation from the next table. He stood up and came over and frowned at me.

"Ashley, aren't you being kind of unfair?" Ross

demanded. "You can't blame Dana just because we lost today. It happens."

Dana squeezed his hand. "Oh, thank you, Ross." She sniffed. "I really appreciate your support."

She reached up and pretended to wipe some tears from her eyes.

What a phony!

"But, Ross—" I protested.

"I mean, you can't beat up on a team member for missing one little crummy shot," Ross went on.

I had heard enough. I scooted back my chair and rose to my feet. "You don't know how wrong you are," I burst out at Ross. "You two deserve each other!" And with that, I ran out of the dining room, trying not to let anyone see that *I* was the one with real tears in my eyes.

Dear Diary,

Poor Ashley! At dinner she and  Dana had a huge fight about the volleyball competition. Ross got in the middle of it, and Dana somehow managed to get him to take her side. Ashley was so upset, she went running out of there.

I got up and started to chase after her. But guess who stopped me?

"Oh, Mary-Kaaaaate!" Jeremy called over from his table. "I need you to do me a favour."

"Not now, Jeremy," I replied, speed-walking to the door. "Ashley needs me!"

"Well, *I* need you more," he said, narrowing his eyes. "Have you forgotten about our little deal?"

I forced myself to do a U-turn and go over to his table. "*What*? What do you want?" I said, clenching my fists.

"I'm having a hard time playing Viper III and eating dinner at the same time," Jeremy explained, pointing to his GameMan. "I need you to feed me my hot dog so I can keep playing."

"No way!"

"I don't think 'no' is an option. Do you, M.K.?"

I gritted my teeth and sat down next to him. I picked up his hot dog and held it up to his mouth.

Elise, Cheryl, and Summer were watching me from the next table. Elise whispered something to Cheryl and Summer, and they all started giggling.

"Put more relish on that first, Mary-Kate," Jeremy ordered. He pressed a couple of buttons on his GameMan. "Come on, die, you viper!"

This is what humiliation is, I thought. *Hand-feeding hot dogs to Jeremy while all your friends watch.*

I had definitely hit rock bottom. It was time for drastic measures.

Chapter 12

Wednesday

Dear Diary,

When I woke up this morning, the first thing I thought was: *at least Dana isn't on the water-skiing team. So she can't mess up the water-skiing competition today.*

Well, guess what, Diary? I was totally wrong!

The water-skiing competition is divided into three parts: jumps, tricks, and the slalom course. After breakfast, about ten minutes before the jumps portion was set to begin, Summer came running up to me on the beach. She looked all panicky.

"Bad news!" she announced.

"You broke a nail," I teased her.

"I did?" Summer held up her nails and studied them.

"No, no, I was just joking . . . What's up, Summer?"

"Cheryl just fell down the stairs and sprained her wrist!" she announced.

"*What?*" I cried out. "Is she okay?"

"Her wrist's all black and blue and yucky," Summer replied, making a face. "Mrs. Clare is taking her to the doctor."

My mind was racing. Cheryl was on the water-skiing team. Without her, we were one team member short. I had to replace her ASAP.

I checked off my options in my head. The water-skiing team consisted of Devon, Mary-Kate, Summer, Jeremy, and me. I tried to remember what had happened during the water-skiing tryouts last Thursday.

Oh, yeah.

Oh, NO!

The only other person who even knew how to water-ski was . . . Dana!

Not only was she a pretty mediocre water-skier, but she was on a mission to make my life miserable!

Dana was incredibly smug when I asked her to fill in for Cheryl. "Oh, so *now* you're begging me to be on the water-skiing team," she said.

I had to bite my lip to keep from saying anything.

"Go ahead, beg," she insisted.

I took a deep breath and counted to ten. Think of  the team, I told myself. Think of the manatees. Think of all the money that's going to go towards saving Florida wildlife. "Please, Dana," I forced myself to say in a sweet, pleading voice. "We really need you on the water-skiing team. Okay?"

Dana tossed her hair over her shoulders. "Oh, okay. If you put it that way." She rushed off to change into her bathing suit.

While we were all waiting for her to come back, Devon marched up to me. "What's going on? I heard Cheryl was out."

"Dana's taking her place," I told him.

I must have looked pretty unhappy, because Devon said, "What's the matter? She knows how to water-ski, right?"

"Sort of."

"Then what's the problem?"

I told him what the problem was. I told him that I was afraid she'd sabotage the water-skiing competition, just like she'd done with the volleyball competition yesterday.

When I was finished, Devon nodded. "Don't worry – I'll take care of it."

"You'll take care of it? How?" I demanded.

"Just leave it to me."

Dana came back a few minutes later, dressed in a black tank suit. "Okay, surf's up or whatever. I'm ready!" she announced.

"Hey, Dana," Devon said, grinning widely at her. "I'll make you a bet."

Dana's eyes flashed. "Bet? What bet?"

"I bet I can beat you in jumps, tricks, *and* slalom," Devon said.

"Oh, no way!" Dana laughed and shook her head. "I'm going to beat *you*, hands down. Just you watch. What are we betting?"

"Loser has to buy the winner the new 4-You CD."

I stifled a gasp. Devon didn't even *like* 4-You!

"Oooh, I don't have that yet!" Dana exclaimed. "You're on!"

Devon flashed me a smile as we picked up our water skis and headed off to join the other schools. I smiled back at him. Who cared if he didn't like 4-You or mint chocolate-chip ice cream? For today, anyway, he was my hero!

Dear Diary,

Guess what? We came in first place in the water-skiing competition! White Oak and Harrington rule!

The entire team pulled off stellar performances at jumps, tricks, and slalom. Even Dana was in top form. I wonder what got into her? She was acting like Queen of the Waves.

Ashley was soooo psyched. She said that all we have to do now is win the 10K bike race tomorrow.

If we can pull that off, we'll place first overall – and we'll get to go to Seaquarium!

I was pretty psyched about our big victory today, too. Until Jeremy came up to me and handed me his water skis and yucky, drippy wetsuit.

"Carry these for me, M.K.," he commanded. "I'm going to go to the hotel gift shop to pick out some postcards. Why don't you meet me in my room in, say . . . fifteen minutes? I'll need you to take dictation."

"Dictation?" I repeated dumbly. "What for?"

"Postcards," Jeremy replied. "Mom and Dad get really annoyed if I don't write to them once a day. I'll dictate, and you can write down what I say."

I gritted my teeth. "Fine."

I dropped Jeremy's water skis and wetsuit off in the locker room area, then went up to his room. I was about to knock when Justin opened the door. He and Jeremy were roommates on this trip.

He smiled at me. "Hey, what's up?"

"Is Jeremy here?" I asked him.

"No, but you can wait for him," Justin said. "I'm going down to the lobby to get some soda. You want anything?"

"No, thanks."

Justin took off down the hall. I went inside their room and shut the door.

Right then I realised how I was going to get out of my horrible, terrible dilemma.

Without wasting another minute I started rifling through Jeremy's stuff. "Okay, Diary, where are you?" I said to myself.

He had to be hiding it somewhere. And if I could just get my hands on it, I would be home free! Jeremy couldn't blackmail me anymore. He could still *tell* people what I wrote, but without the diary, he wouldn't have any proof. No one would ever believe him!

I dug through his suitcase, his backpack, his dirty laundry. I searched under his bed, through his dressing table drawers, and in every nook and cranny.

There was no sign of my diary anywhere.

I was just about to give up when I felt something under Jeremy's pillow. I pulled it out. It was a diary!

But it wasn't *my* diary. On the cover, it said: JEREMY BURKE'S EXCELLENT DIARY.

Holy cow! I thought, grinning from ear to ear. *Maybe THIS is my ticket to freedom!*

Chapter 13

Thursday

Dear Diary,

I woke up this morning in a cold sweat.

This was the day. This was the day we were going to have to win the 10K.

Sunlight streamed through our curtains. Mary-Kate was still asleep. She was snoring and mumbling under the covers.

I went over to her bed and tapped her on the shoulder. "Hey, Mary-Kate. Wake up!"

"Hmmm? Jeremy? Your socks are almost dry. What do you want, scrambled eggs or sunny-side-up? Let me just sleep for a second. . . ."

I shook Mary-Kate harder. "Mary-Kate, wake up! You're having a bad dream."

Mary-Kate's eyes flew open. "What? Oh, hey, Ashley. Is it morning?"

"Uh-huh." I stared at my sister. "Okay, I can't stand it anymore. 'Fess up. *What* is going on with you and Jeremy?"

Mary-Kate looked scared. "What do you mean?"

"I mean, you've been acting totally bizarre for the last few days. You bring him all his meals, you hand-feed him hot dogs, and you're doing his laundry. Not to mention the fact that you set up all those shots for him in volleyball, and you carried his water-skiing stuff. What's up?"

Mary-Kate sighed miserably. "Okay, I'll tell you. But you have to promise not to tell anyone – especially Jeremy!"

I held up my right hand. "I swear. Twin's honour."

Mary-Kate sighed again. "When Phoebe and I were stranded in the swamp, we were kind of thinking that we might not make it back," she explained. "So we wrote this thing in my diary called the Last Will and Testament. We left stuff for all our friends."

"That's kind of depressing," I remarked.

"Well, a lot of it was a joke. We left all kinds of *mean* stuff for our friends. And we wrote mean things about them." She paused. "Anyway, remember when I told you that I lost my diary somewhere between Camp Coral Reef and here?"

"Uh-huh."

"It turned out that Jeremy had it! And he's been blackmailing me!"

I gasped.

"He said he'd tell all my friends what I wrote about them unless I did whatever he asked," Mary-Kate went on.

I rolled my eyes. "Oh, brother. That explains a lot!"

Two for the Road

Mary-Kate's eyes gleamed. "The thing is, I found his diary. I'm going to use it to get *my* diary back."

"Way to go, sis!" I grinned.

I think Mary-Kate felt a lot better telling me all this. I gave her a hug and told her everything was going to be fine. She was never going to have to be Jeremy's personal maid again.

But at the moment I had to get ready for the big 10K!

I put on my bike shorts and top and headed downstairs. After a quick breakfast I went out to the starting line. While I was doing my stretches, the rest of my team showed up: Phoebe, Ross, Dana, Elise, and Seth.

I thought I saw Ross sneak a look at me. Was it my new SAVE THE MANATEES tank top? Or my amazing leadership skills? Either way, my heart did a little dance. But then Dana came up and pulled him off to look at her bicycle tyres.

Maybe Ross was ready to be friendly again. But now was not the time to think about this. I had to concentrate on the race.

The other schools were starting to gather around. Angela announced over the megaphone that the race would be starting in a few minutes.

I got my team into a huddle and gave everyone a pep talk.

"Okay, if we win this one, we'll get the big prize!" I cried out. "Let's go! We can do it!"

Everyone joined hands and then burst out of the huddle with a big cheer. We strapped on our helmets, straddled our bikes, and rode over to the starting line.

"On your marks, get set . . . GO!" Angela blew the whistle. The race was starting! We all squeezed our handlebars and tucked our heads and rode into the wind.

A salty breeze whipped my hair around. I could hear chains clanking and wheels turning all around me. I tried not to get psyched out by the fact that there were so many kids riding next to me, behind me, and in front of me. I just tried to focus on pumping my legs as hard as I could.

The course took us up the beach, through a big park, and back again. People cheered all along the way. Seagulls swooped through the air.

By the 9K mark, Phoebe, Ross, Elise, and Seth were way up front, along with half a dozen kids from other schools. I was somewhere in the middle. Dana was lagging behind. Was she doing it on purpose? I pedalled extra-hard, trying to shave every extra second off my time so I could make up for Dana. At the end of the race the team with the lowest combined score would win.

I saw the finish line up ahead. Almost there!

And then my front tyre hit a rock.

My bike jerked violently. I wasn't prepared. The next thing I knew, I flew into the air and landed on the pavement, hard.

I heard other bikes whizzing past me. I tried to get up, but I couldn't stand on my ankle. Tears stung my eyes. Had I sprained it? Was I not going to be able to finish the race?

A bike screeched to a halt in front of me. I looked up and saw Dana turning around. She hesitated a moment, as if she were trying to decide what to do.

She got off her bike and ran over. "Ashley, are you okay?"

"It-it's my ankle," I told her. "I-I think it might be sprained."

"Try to stand up," she said.

She held my hand and helped me to my feet.

I put some weight on the bad ankle. It hurt, but it wasn't excruciating.

"You think you can finish?" Dana asked me.

"I'm not sure."

She flipped her hair over her shoulders. "Come on, I'll help you."

She put her arm around me and got me back up on my bike. "Easy now," she said. "Pedal with your good foot. Let the other one just kind of rest."

I did what she said. She rode beside me for the last fifteen yards.

And just like that, Dana and I crossed the finish line – side by side.

The rest of our team came running to us.

"Are you all right, Ashley?" Phoebe demanded.

"Dana, you saved her!" Summer exclaimed.

Dana grinned. "Oh, it was nothing. I do stuff like that all the time."

I could tell Dana liked being the centre of attention. She *always* liked being the centre of attention. But who was I to hold it against her? She really did save me.

And, as it turned out, she saved the race!

When the last cyclists had crossed the finish line, Angela figured out everyone's times. "The White Oak-Harrington team is the winner of the 10K!" she announced. "That also means that they win the tournament!"

Ross, Phoebe, Seth, Elise, Dana, and I screamed and grabbed one another in a big group hug. Mary-Kate, Cheryl, and everyone else came running up to us and joined the group hug, too. "We did it! We did it!" we all shouted.

My ankle still hurt, but my heart was pounding with happiness. Seaquarium, here we come! And I owed it all to Dana. Can you believe it, Diary?

Dear Diary,

Guess what? I was getting ready for the big victory party on the beach. I wanted to wear my favourite pink earrings, the ones with the crystal hearts dangling from them. Ashley gave them to me for my birthday last year.

I couldn't find one of them, though. I searched everywhere. But no earring.

I decided to check my suit-case. I ran my hand all over the lining, in case the earring had fallen into a crack or something.

Sure enough, there was the earring. And guess what else I found?

My diary!

It had somehow slipped through a tear in the lining and lodged itself way deep. I was so relieved . . .

And then I was *furious*!

Because this meant that Jeremy never had my diary to begin with! He made it all up, just so he could blackmail me into being his personal maid.

My mind was racing. On Wednesday, when everyone was hanging out at the pool, I complained to Phoebe about the missing diary. While we were talking, I thought I heard something – or someone – in the bushes. It must have been Jeremy, eavesdropping on us!

It took him less than forty-eight hours to figure out what to do with the info. On Friday he left me the first note.

I stared out of the window at the beach, where Angela and Mrs. Clare were starting a bonfire for the victory party.

"All right, Jeremy," I said, rubbing my hands together. "It's payback time!"

Chapter 14

Thursday

Dear Diary,

Life is good. No, I take that back, Diary. Life is totally, completely awesome!

We had our victory party tonight. There was a bonfire, and a barbecue, and lots of music and dancing on the beach. I couldn't do any dancing, though. My ankle was all taped up – just like Cheryl's wrist.

"I guess we're the two casualties," Cheryl said.

"But it was worth it! We won!" Cheryl and I laughed and exchanged high fives on that.

Just then, Ross came up to us. I stopped in the middle of my high five and glanced at him in surprise. "Hey."

"Hey, Ashley." He sat down beside me on my beach blanket. Cheryl mumbled something about having to grab some dessert, then scurried away.

"How's it going?" I asked him.

Ross shrugged. "Okay."

He looked like he wanted to say something. I smiled at him and waited.

"So, listen," Ross said after a minute. "I know everyone thinks Dana's a big hero because she saved you and all that." He hesitated. "But I just wanted to tell you *you're* the real hero. You were a great team captain. Without you we probably wouldn't have won first place."

I could feel myself blushing. And smiling. And blushing some more. "Thanks, Ross," I said.

"You're welcome," Ross said. "How's your ankle?"

"Better. It wasn't a really bad sprain."

"Let me see."

He bent down and took my ankle in his hands. He peeked under the Ace bandage. "Doesn't look too bad."

His hands on my ankle were making it hard for me to think straight. Or talk. At that moment my entire vocabulary had disappeared from my brain.

Ross let go of my ankle and gazed into my eyes. "Ashley, I've missed you . . ." he began.

"I've missed you, too," I blurted out.

 He reached over and gave me a hug. My heart totally melted. Ross and I were a couple again!

We spent the rest of the evening holding hands and talking.

Two for the Road

We had so much to catch up on. We even slow-danced to one song, with me hobbling on my bad ankle.

Didn't I tell you life was totally, completely awesome, Diary?

Dear Diary (my *real* diary),

Jeremy didn't know what hit him.

During the victory party, I kept messing up his orders.

"M.K., I told you to get me ginger ale, not punch," Jeremy snapped.

"What? Oh. Sorry 'bout that, Jeremy."

"And where are my barbecued ribs?"

"Hmmmm? In a minute, okay? I'm busy."

After an hour of this, Jeremy called me aside. "What's going on?" he demanded. "If you don't shape up, you know what's going to happen. I'm going to read your diary out loud, right here and now!"

"I'm sorry," I said innocently. "It won't happen again."

While we were all chowing down on toasted marshmallows, Ashley hobbled up to the front of the crowd with Angela's megaphone.

"Speech!" Seth and Justin yelled. Everyone broke into applause.

Ashley grinned and waved. "I just wanted to thank you all for being such an awesome team," she said.

More applause.

"Because of your hard work and dedication, our sponsors are donating a thousand dollars to the Wildlife Fund," Ashley went on. "Plus, we get to go to Seaquarium tomorrow and hang out with dolphins and manatees!"

Everyone cheered.

"That's all. Anyone else want to make a speech?" Ashley smiled and waved the megaphone around. Ross took it and got up to thank Mrs. Clare.

I quietly pulled Jeremy's diary out of my backpack. I opened it to the middle and leaned over to Jeremy.

"What do you think, Jer? Should I go up there and read everyone a page from your excellent diary?" I whispered. "Listen, here's a good one. 'Dear Diary. I think I'm over my stupid crush on Dana Woletsky. But maybe not. Do you think I should ask her to the Homecoming Dance, Diary? She might hold it against me that I'm Ashley and Mary-Kate's cousin. On the other hand, I could wear my lucky socks when I ask her. That might give me an edge.'"

Jeremy lunged at me. "Give me that!"

"You never *did* have my diary, did you?" I said. "You're lucky I didn't just give your diary to Phoebe! She could have published it in the *Acorn*!"

Jeremy grabbed his diary from me and stomped off. His face was as red as a lobster.

Justice. It was a good feeling.

Chapter 15

Saturday

Dear Diary,

Today we went to the Seaquarium. Diary, it was amazing!

There were all kinds of awesome fish there, including tropical fish of every colour of the rainbow. We got to see sharks being fed. We saw stingrays and barracudas, too. We even got to touch a bunch of stuff, including starfish, sea cucumbers, and hermit crabs! Super-slimy!

The twelve of us, plus Mrs. Clare, were given VIP treatment. A special tour guide, Tico, took us all around. He showed us a special film about Florida ecology. He told us all kinds of cool stories about the different sea creatures.

Ross stayed by my side the whole time. We held hands and talked about the rest of the summer.

"I'll miss you," he told me.

"I'll miss you, too," I told him. "Let's e-mail each other every day!"

"Definitely! And I'll see if my parents will let me visit my cousin in Chicago," Ross promised.

My heart skipped a beat. "That would be great."

At the end of the day we got to put on our swimming suits and splash around in the pool with the dolphins. There was a whole family of them. One of them even kissed me on the nose!

The best part was when we got to meet the baby manatee! It was soft and brown and had a sweet face, kind of like a walrus's. Its mom was huge and kept nudging the baby under the water. But the baby kept popping up and blinking at us with its big brown eyes.

Our tour guide, Tico, turned to us. "So what do you think you all want to name it?" he asked us. "That's part of your prize!"

"How about Emily Dickinson?" Phoebe suggested. Emily Dickinson was Phoebe's favourite poet.

"How about Fluffy?" Summer said.

"How about Dana?" Dana said.

I raised my hand. "How about Victory?"

Everyone liked that. "Victory it is," Tico said. He smiled at the baby manatee. "Hey, Victory, welcome to the world!"

Victory blinked at us and splashed around in the water. I squeezed Ross's hand. This was the best summer vacation ever!

Two of a Kind Diaries

Dear New Diary,

Last night I decided to throw the Last Will and Testament pages from my diary in the bonfire. They were too dangerous to keep around.

Now I'm writing in my new diary. It was time for a fresh start! It's a cool-looking notebook I got today at Seaquarium, with a picture of manatees on the cover.

What lesson did I learn from all this? Never write mean stuff about your friends. Even if your diary doesn't end up disappearing.

Ashley's across the room, packing her suitcase. She looks annoyed because she can't cram everything in. I guess she bought too many souvenirs!

We're leaving first thing tomorrow for Miami airport. And then it's home to Chicago, and Dad, and all our friends there. I can't wait!

I'm going to miss Miami and the manatees. I'm also going to miss all our friends. We won't see each other for the rest of the summer.

But then we'll all be back together this fall when school starts again. I wonder what the new year will be like? After what we've been through these last four weeks in Florida, New Hampshire's going to seem pretty tame.

Or will it?

PSST! Take a sneak peek at

Surprise, Surprise!

There was a knock on the dorm room door. Mary-Kate opened it.

Rebecca Duncan was standing there with one hand on her hips – and a half-eaten jumble crumble bar in the other. "Your jumble things are too chewy," she said, thrusting the bar at Mary-Kate. "I can't eat this. The caramel corn is totally sticking to my teeth!"

"Oh . . . uh, sorry," Mary-Kate said. "Uh, I think the next batch will be better. I'll give you another one tomorrow. Free."

"No thanks," Rebecca said. "I think I want my money back." She turned and glanced over her shoulder, into the hall. "And so do they!"

What? Mary-Kate's heart started pounding. She jumped up off her bed. *Who?*

But as soon as she reached the door, she saw the answer. There were five other people lined up outside her room!

"Sorry, but we can't eat these things," Elise complained, holding her half-eaten bar out to Mary-Kate. "It's like chewing dried glue!"

"Okay, okay," Mary-Kate said, holding up her hands. "Never mind. I'll give you your money back."

She almost wanted to cry as she stood in the hall, passing out dollar bills. When it was over, she had given back twenty-three of the twenty-four dollars she had earned on that batch.

Why not all twenty-four? she wondered. At least someone must have liked my jumble crumble bars.

She hurried down the hall to Ashley's room. Ashley was sitting at her desk working on her homework.

"Ashley, you've got to help me," Mary-Kate begged, racing into the room. "My cookies are a disaster. If I can't sell enough of them, I'll never be able to buy a snowboard in time to play on the Winter Sports team."

Ashley shook her head. "Sorry, but I've got homework. Tons. And I'll probably still be working on the fashion column for the *Acorn*. I really wish I could help you out, Mary-Kate – honestly I do. But I'm swamped."

Mary-Kate started to leave the room.

Then she noticed something in the wastebasket beside Phoebe's desk. It was a jumble crumble bar – with one bite taken out of it.

"What's that?" Mary-Kate asked, pointing into the trash.

"Oh, Phoebe bought it from Elliot," Ashley explained. "She couldn't eat it – but she didn't want to hurt your feelings."

"So that's where the last one went," Mary-Kate mumbled, feeling worse than ever.

And that's where my dreams of getting a snowboard are going, too, she thought.

Straight into the trash!

mary-kateandashley

TWO of a kind ™

(1) It's a Twin Thing (0 00 714480 6)

(2) How to Flunk Your First Date (0 00 714479 2)

(3) The Sleepover Secret (0 00 714478 4)

(4) One Twin Too Many (0 00 714477 6)

(5) To Snoop or Not to Snoop? (0 00 714476 8)

(6) My Sister the Supermodel (0 00 714475 X)

(7) Two's a Crowd (0 00 714474 1)

(8) Let's Party! (0 00 714473 3)

(9) Calling All Boys (0 00 714472 5)

(10) Winner Take All (0 00 714471 7)

(11) P.S. Wish You Were Here (0 00 714470 9)

(12) The Cool Club (0 00 714469 5)

(13) War of the Wardrobes (0 00 714468 7)

(14) Bye-bye Boyfriend (0 00 714467 9)

(15) It's Snow Problem (0 00 714466 0)

(16) Likes Me, Likes Me Not (0 00 714465 2)

(17) Shore Thing (0 00 714464 4)

(18) Two for the Road (0 00 714463 6)

(19) Surprise, Surprise! (0 00 714462 8)

(20) Sealed With a Kiss (0 00 714461 X)

(21) Now You See Him, Now You Don't (0 00 714446 6)

HarperCollins*Entertainment*

DUALSTAR PUBLICATIONS

mary-kateandashley.com
AOL Keyword: mary-kateandashley

PARACHUTE PRESS

TM & © 2002 Dualstar Entertainment Group, LLC.

mary-kateandashley

mary-kateandashley

Sweet 16

(1) *Never Been Kissed*   (0 00 714879 8)
(2) *Wishes and Dreams*   (0 00 714880 1)
(3) *The Perfect Summer*   (0 00 714881 X)

HarperCollins*Entertainment*

PARACHUTE PRESS

DUALSTAR PUBLICATIONS

mary-kateandashley.com
AOL Keyword: mary-kateandashley

Real Books for Real Girls

b the 1st 2 kno
mary-kateandashley

It's What **YOU** Read

REGISTER 4 THE HARPERCOLLINS AND MK&ASH TEXT CLUB AND KEEP UP2 D8 WITH THE L8EST MK&ASH BOOK NEWS AND MORE.

SIMPLY TEXT TOK, FOLLOWED BY YOUR GENDER (M/F), DATE OF BIRTH (DD/MM/YY) AND POSTCODE TO: 07786277301.

SO, IF YOU ARE A GIRL BORN ON THE 12TH MARCH 1986 AND LIVE IN THE POSTCODE DISTRICT RG19 YOUR MESSAGE WOULD LOOK LIKE THIS: TOKF120386RG19.

IF YOU ARE UNDER 14 YEARS WE WILL NEED YOUR PARENTS'' OR GUARDIANS'' PERMISSION FOR US TO CONTACT YOU. PLEASE ADD THE LETTER 'G'' TO THE END OF YOUR MESSAGE TO SHOW YOU HAVE YOUR PARENTS'' CONSENT. LIKE THIS: TOKF120386RG19G.

HarperCollins*Entertainment*

PARACHUTE PRESS

DUALSTAR PUBLICATIONS

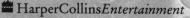
mary-kateandashley.com
AOL Keyword: mary-kateandashley

TM & © 2002 Dualstar Entertainment Group, LLC.